A Note to Parents & Caregivers—

Reading Stars books are designed to build confidence in the earliest of readers. Relying on word repetition and visual cues, each book features less than 50 words.

You can help your child develop a lifetime love of reading right from the very start. Here are some ways to help your beginning reader get going:

⭐ Read the book aloud as a first introduction

⭐ Run your fingers below the words as you read each line

⭐ Give your child the chance to finish the sentences or read repeating words while you read the rest.

⭐ Encourage your child to read aloud every day!

Every Child can be a Reading Star!

Published in the United States by Xist Publishing
www.xistpublishing.com
PO Box 61593 Irvine, CA 92602

© 2019 Text Copyright Juliana O'Neill
Illustration by Sergo77
Licensed from Adobe Stock and edited by Xist Publishing

First Edition
ISBN: 978-1-5324-1263-9
eISBN: 978-1-5324-1262-2

Say Boo

Juliana O'Neill

xist Publishing

Say Boo to
the witch.

5

Say Boo to
the ghost.

8

Say Boo on
the night

I love the most.

Say Boo with your costume.

13

14

Say Boo with some treats.

16

Say Boo and
remember

To be scary
and sweet.

20

Say Boo with your family.

Say Boo with

your friends.

BOO!

Say Boo, it's a party

That reminds
of our ends.

I am a Reading Star because I can read the words in this book:

a	our
and	party
be	remember
boo	reminds
costume	say
ends	scary
family	some
friends	sweet
ghost	that
I	the
it's	to
love	treats
most	witch
night	with
of	your
on	

CPSIA information can be obtained
at www.ICGtesting.com
Printed in the USA
BVHW092135120219
540133BV00004B/44/P